A SQUARE IN A SQUARE® PATTERN BOOK
THE 2ND IN THE SERIES

By Jodi Barrows

1613 Lost Lake Drive • Keller, Texas 76248

TOLL FREE 1-888-624-6260   FAX 817-605-7420

EMAIL qyjodi@yahoo.com

WEB www.squareinasquare.com

Liz's Mercantile

A SQUARE IN A SQUARE® PATTERN BOOK

By Jodi Barrows

CREDITS:

This book is dedicated to the certified teachers. Thank you ladies! You are talented, sweet friends!
Paula Doll, Sharon Hill, Janice Sutton, Jean Kearney, Janet Blazekovich, Barbara Handler, Kay Roberts, Bonnie Taylor, Kristi Droese, Peg Oppenheimer, Judy Chambers, Laurie Kral, Kathy Kuryla, Helen Ray, Janie Alonzo, Crescent Clark, Julie Jenkins, Janet Scheer, and Bonnie Walker.
There are many more, but these are the ones that came to Texas to work on this book.

Quilt piecing, support and testing:
Kay Roberts, Julie Jenkins, Helen Kay, Janie Alonzo, Judy Chambers, Laurie Kral, Linda Watts

Machine quilting:
JaLonn Carter-Stanley, Julie Jenkins

Book Proofing:
Square in a Square® Certified Teachers:

Barbara Handler, Kay Roberts, Bonnie Taylor, Peg Oppenheimer, Laurie Kral, Gail Otke
Kathy Kuryla, Janie Alonzo, Julie Jenkins, Kristi Droese, Bonnie Walker, Judy Chambers, Janet Scheer.

Office Support:
Steve Barrows, Jenny Sinlgeton, LindaWatts

Graphic Design: Rita Frank, Grand Junction, CO
Printing: Branch Smith Printing, Fort Worth, TX
Photography: Holly Perez, Fort Worth, TX

ISBN-13: 978-0-9766858-3-8
ISBN-10: 0-9766858-3-3

1st Printing

CONTENTS

Introduction 3
Tips & Hints 4
General Directions 5
Crosscut 4-Patch 6
Crosscut 9-Patch 7
4 Patch, 9 Patch Chart 8
Basic Steps 9
Option #1 10
Option #3 11
Option #4 12
Option #5 13
Option #11 14
Option #14 15
Option #16 16
Basic Diamond Cuttinig & Sewing 17
Option #18 18
Option #19 19-20
Option #20 21-22
Setting Triangle Chart 27
Binding 28-29
Patterns
  1. Split Bear Paw 30-31
  2. Mrs. Sewell's Star 32-33
  3. Peddler's Choice 34-35
  4. Lickety Split 36
  5. Monkey Tails 37-38
  6. Timber Trails 39
  7. Homestead Star 40-41
  8. Emma's Crossroads 42-43
  9. Abby's Basket Sampler 44-46
  10. Indian Blanket 47-48

Are you on our list to receive our newsletter by email?
If not, please call or email:
1-888-624-6260 • qyjodi@yahoo.com

INTRODUCTION

Liz's Mercantile

Liz's Mercantile is the second book in our series. Each series consists of the Pattern book, novel and fabric collection.

Our story started in 1856 with our family of women leaving their Riverton home in Louisiana and going west.

If this is your first opportunity to know about our series you can get caught up on the family in the "Leaving Riverton" series of pattern book, novel and fabric.

The women are all from my family and the situation is true to our family history.

Be sure to check out Liz's Mercantile the sequel novel as well. The women make it to Fort Worth, Texas. But their troubles aren't over yet! We have some new characters introduced in the story sweet Anna Parker the pastor's wife, wily Samuel Smith a Fort Worth resident. The county peddler Mr. Skelly is back with his lively Irish brogue. Thomas gives Liz an ultimatum and waits until sunup for the answer; the women stand over a new grave in the Texas earth; their courage and perseverance are tested again and again. In all of this they produce beautiful quilts by lamp lights with limited convenience or resources. Joy and sorrow are all woven together in each and every stitch of the women's needle.

Some of the quilts in this book were pieced and quilted by my talented certified teachers. Our cover quilt "Mrs. Sewell's Stars" was pieced by Kay Roberts of Tennessee and quilted by Jalonne Carter-Stanley of Texas.

Grandpa Lucas' quilt "Timber Trails" was pieced by a sister team Helen Ray and Janie Alsonso both of Texas.

Luke's quilt "Split Bear Paw" was pieced by Judy Chambers of Florida and quilted by Jalonne Carter-Stanley of Texas.

Peddlers Choice - Mr. Skelly's Quilt was pieced and quilted by Julie Jenkins of Wisconsin.

Emma's Crossroads quilt was pieced by Linda Watts and quilted by Jalonne Carter-Stanly both of north Texas.

The rest of the quilts were pieced by me and quilted by Jalonne.

Remember to look at these quilts with a new eye. With the Square in a Square construction, NO triangle is a problem. All quilts are made with the basic square and strips on each side. The way you trim defines it as a triangle unit or option. It really is simple, fast and easy! The quilts can be pieced together in record time with all points sharp and precise and no ripping to achieve perfection!

All of the quilts in this book were made from the Leaving Riverton, Liz's Mercantile and the Liz's Plaid Fabric Collections. Check your favorite quilt shop or our website to purchase these collections. The plaids and black toiles were so new at this printing we didn't even have code numbers yet!

The charts help you when you wish to adapt the options or triangle units to other designs. The pattern will tell you exactly what size and color of strips & squares to cut.

Now with the fabric line readily available even color is easy and quick.

Any of the fabric can be ordered on-line or by phone. The numbers keep it simple. Kits may already be ready. Be sure to check the slide shows or photo galleries on the web for additional color choices.

If you ever have questions or need help adapting, just contact us. We are here to help you succeed and become a quilt pro with out the hassle! Anyone can start with this book and learn the System!

$\mathcal{T}$IPS & HINTS

- The Magic Math is only needed when you create a design from scratch.

- Remember to sew a "scant" 1/4" seam.

- Spray starch helps to keep washed fabric from moving.

- A finger space between the square on the strip is all that's needed, when sewing the basic square.

- Blunt corners are good, on some options.

- Use short strips on side 3 and side 4 when sewing the basic square or basic diamond.

- If your option is too large or small, check:

    1. center square size

    2. seam allowance

    3. the way you lay your ruler on the sewn square

- Place strip in your machine first with diamond on top, right sides together.

- Handle fabric carefully. Don't pull or stretch.

- Don't overwork the fabric units when pressing.

- Seams may be pressed open.

- Test one block before cutting the entire quilt.

- Multiple pieces or small units are easier with this technqiue and system. Lots of seams take more time, but are not more difficult.

- Use a stilletto to help with thickness and fabric direction.

- A single hole throat plate on the sewing machine helps with small units with a straight stitch.

- Try the 3 new perfecting patchwork tools: Crosscut 4-Patch™, Crosscut 9-Patch™ and the smaller new Square in a Square® which is easier to handle.

- Remember to press blocks so that they press flat. This will help you remember to press to the least amount of seams, or so that individual option units are flat.

- The charts and information are all here to help you be creative with your block building. If you are confused by too much information, just follow the block information or pattern information where we have done all of the work for you.

- Notice there will be an S or F by some measurements. The trimming requirements for the Option #19 will be a 3/16" on the North and South side. It is difficult to create an exact and easy measurement. 3/16 is 3 or 4 threads. That is the thickness of a cutting line on a tool. The S means scant cut. The F equals a full cut. To make a full cut it would be on the outside of the cutting line to make the size larger. Of course providing that your cutting and sewing is perfect. Remember the size of your units depend on 3 things: the size of your center unit of the option, your seam allowance all figured on a scant or skinny 1/4", and lastly, the way you lay the cutting tool on the sewn piece. Are you cutting with the line to create a scant or skinny cut or a full and fat cut. Have fun with which ever you choose. The perfection is here for you Rocket Science quilters. The technqiue is forgiving for the Smoking Needle quilter.

- If you are following one of our Square in a Square® patterns you do not need any of the Magic Math™ or charts. Just start cutting and sewing with Step 1.

- Strips are cut selvedge to selvedge.

- SnS equals Square in a Square®.

- Most of the time the size you are looking for is on the chart. You only need the Magic Math™ if it is an unusual size.

As always, I consider my books to be workbooks. I have given you lots of information to help you be creative.

Cutting

You will be cutting strips of fabric from yardage or fat quarters. Cutting instructions are given for full widths, 42" - 44". If using fat quarters, simply cut twice as many strips as stated. Fold or layer the fabric. Make a clean up cut on one

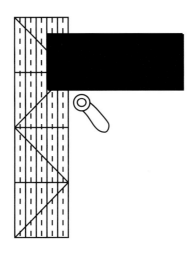

edge. You can cut about six layers at once. More than that is risky, as the fabric shifts.

Often the directions call for crosscuts. These are made of strips or strip sets (strips sewn together).

Machine Piecing

Machine piecing is strong, fast and accurate. Learn to sew a 1/4" seam; it is a must. To test your 1/4" seam, stitch together three 1-1/2" x 6" strips along the 6" edge. Press. The unit will measure 3-1/2" x 6" if the seam allowance is accurate. If it doesn't, practice until it does.

For more accurate piecing, try using spray starch on the fabric before sewing. This is very helpful with miniatures or with pre washed fabric.

When you have two pieces that should fit together, but don't, you will have to ease them. Pin them well and make them fit so seams and points will match up. The fullest piece should

3-1/2"

feed through the machine on the bottom. The feed dogs will help ease the fullness more evenly and the foot on top will slightly pull the top layer.

Chain Piecing

Chain piecing has always been a natural for me. I did it before I knew someone else had invented it! Keep sewing the units, one after the other, into the machine without lifting the presser foot or cutting threads. When you change to another part of the pattern, or you have about a mile of pieces on the back of your machine, stop and cut them apart, or have the kids help to snip them. I also use a runner, which is a small scrap of fabric. I run it into the machine when I don't have a pattern piece to sew or I need to stop on the chain piecing. It just leaves the machine in neutral, ready to sew. With a runner and chain piecing, you don't have a mess with clipping all of those loose threads, or lift the presser foot.

Square in a Square®

All of the quilts in this book are based on my Square in a Square® (SnS) piecing technique. This method creates squares within each other by sewing strips and squares together. It results in extra clean cuts and accuracy not found with other methods. There are several options to the technique, you will be amazed at how versatile the SnS technique can be.

Basic Steps for Square in a Square®

All of the quilts included give detailed cutting instructions. If you want to design your own quilt, the directions which follow give formulas for calculating measurements. Round to the nearest 1/8". Use the chart below to convert the decimals on the calculator to fractions.

1/8 = .125	5/8 = .625
1/4 = .25	3/4 = .75
3/8 = .375	7/8 = .875
1/2 = .5	

Since there is rounding involved in this technique the following will help you to be more accurate.

When sewing a bias and straight grain edge together, always ease or stretch the bias piece to fit the straight grain piece. Also, whenever possible, sew with straight grain edges on top and bias on the bottom.

About The Ruler

• The first row of numbers on the left is the width of a single cut strip.

• The second row going up the middle is the width of a single strip sewn on one side. One edge is sewn, the other is a raw edge.

• The 3rd row to the right is the cut measurement of the total unit. Strip 1 and 2 have one raw edge and 1 sewn edge.

How to Place the Crosscut 4-Patch Ruler and Make the Crosscut:

Cut the clean up cut along the end of the sewn strip section.

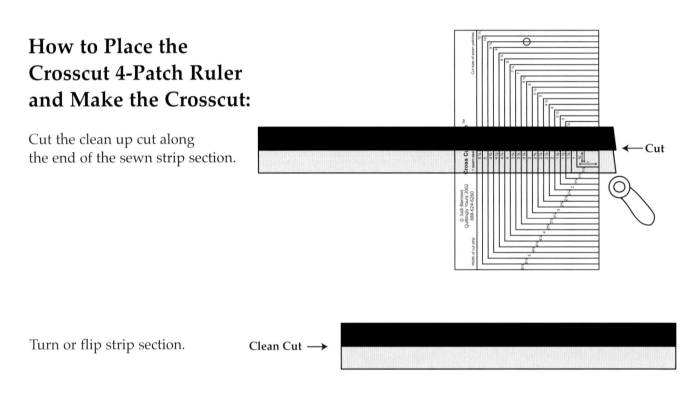

← Cut

Turn or flip strip section.

Clean Cut →

Line up the correct 4-patch unit. The lines will tell you if each cross cut section is perfect.

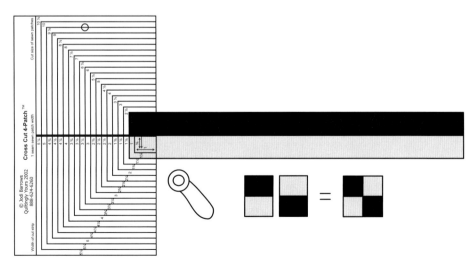

About The Ruler

• The first row of numbers on the left is the width of a single cut strip.

• The second row going up to the left is the width of a single strip sewn on one side to the center strip. One edge is sewn, the other is a raw edge.

• The 3rd row of numbers is the width of the sewn center row of strips. Both sides have a seam.

• The 4th row to the right is the cut measurement of the total unit. Strip 1 and 3 have 1 raw edge and 1 sewn edge. The center strip has a sewn seam on each side.

How to Place the Crosscut 9-Patch Ruler and Make the Crosscut:

Cut the clean up cut along the end of the sewn strip section.

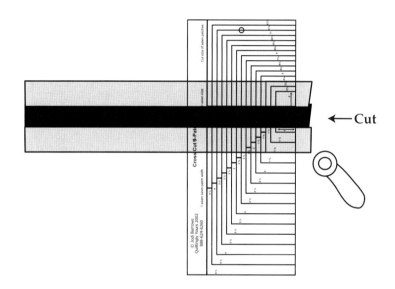

← Cut

Turn or flip strip section.

Clean Cut →

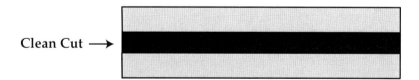

Line up the correct 9-patch unit. The lines will tell you if each cross cut section is perfect.

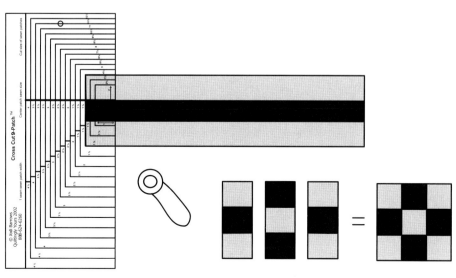

7

4 Patch Chart

A single square is used to create blocks.

A sewn size
B cut size

C block sewn size

D block cut size

A Sewn or Graph Paper size Small Square	B Cut Size of Small Square	C Sewn or Graph Size of Block Square	D Cut Size of Block Square
1/2"	1"	1"	1-1/2"
3/4"	1-1/4"	1-1/2"	2"
1"	1-1/2"	2"	2-1/2"
1-1/4"	1-3/4"	2-1/2"	3"
1-1/2"	2"	3"	3-1/2"
1-3/4"	2-1/4"	3-1/2"	4"
2"	2-1/2"	4"	4-1/2"
2-1/4"	2-3/4"	4-1/2"	5"
2-1/2"	3"	5"	5-1/2"
2-3/4"	3-1/4"	5-1/2"	6"
3"	3-1/2"	6"	6-1/2"
3-1/4"	3-3/4"	6-1/2"	7"
3-1/2"	4"	7"	7-1/2"
3-3/4"	4-1/4"	7-1/2"	8"
4"	4-1/2"	8"	8-1/2"
4-1/4"	4-3/4"	8-1/2"	9"
4-1/2"	5"	9"	9-1/2"
4-3/4"	5-1/4"	9-1/2"	10"
5"	5-1/2"	10"	10-1/2"

9 Patch Chart

A sewn size
B cut size

C block sewn size

D block cut size

A Sewn or Graph Paper size Small Square	B Cut Size of Small Square	C Sewn or Graph Size of Block Square	D Cut Size of Block Square
1/2"	1"	1-1/2"	2"
3/4"	1-1/4"	2-1/4"	2-3/4"
1"	1-1/2"	3"	3-1/2"
1-1/4"	1-3/4"	3-3/4"	4-1/4"
1-1/2"	2"	4-1/2"	5"
1-3/4"	2-1/4"	5-1/4"	5-3/4"
2"	2-1/2"	6"	6-1/2"
2-1/4"	2-3/4"	6-3/4"	7-1/4"
2-1/2"	3"	7-1/2"	8"
2-3/4"	3-1/4"	8-1/4"	8-3/4"
3"	3-1/2"	9"	9-1/2"
3-1/4"	3-3/4"	9-3/4"	10-1/4"
3-1/2"	4"	10-1/2"	11"
3-3/4"	4-1/4"	11-1/4"	11-3/4"
4"	4-1/2"	12"	12-1/2"

You will be making a "Square in a Square®". This is sewing strips and squares together to create squares within each other. When you sew first and then cut the triangles, it allows extra clean cuts, and accurate blocks or units for blocks. No triangle stretch or bias worry. You may cut straight or bias fabric strips. You will be amazed at how versatile this "Square in a Square®" technique can be! Let's get started.

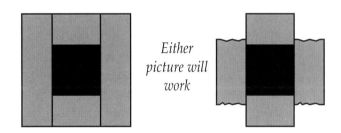

- Lay the corner strip face up on your sewing machine. Place the square face down on the strip with edges even. Sew 1/4" along edge of square. Lay the next square down on the strip and continue on in the chain piecing method.

- Repeat for the opposite side of the square.

- Cut the squares apart and press open – seams out.

- Sew strips to the other two sides of the square

  Hint: *to save fabric, just sew a strip the length of center square plus 1/2"*

- Press open – seams out.

Either picture will work

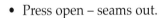

- Cut a "Square in a Square®" block. The "Square in a Square®" ruler makes this step easy. Match the corner on the inside square with the corresponding angle on the ruler. Trim all four corners according to the option you choose. Notice that sometimes the corners are blunted just a little. This won't affect the finished square at all. You now have a "Square in a Square®".

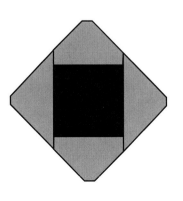

9

$\mathcal{O}$PTION 1

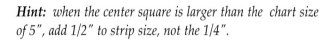

When cutting your "SnS®", leave 1/4" seam allowance on all 4 sides of your square, don't sew or cut off the tip of the inside squares.

Use this math formula to find your strip size:

To find the strip size for the corner, measure center square..... Divide in half....Add 1/4"...... Cut strip this measurement for the next row to sew around your square.

Hint: when the center square is larger than the chart size of 5", add 1/2" to strip size, not the 1/4".

Hint: to save fabric, just sew a strip the length of the center square plus 1/2".

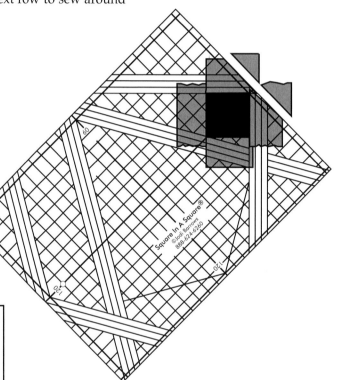

Chart for Option #1
Total Finished Size

Sewn-Finished or Graph Paper Size	Cut Center Square	Cut Strip Size
1	1-1/4	3/4
1-1/4	1-3/8	1
1-1/2	1-5/8	1-1/8
1-3/4	1-3/4	1-1/4
2	2	1-1/4
2-1/4	2-1/8	1-3/8
2-1/2	2-1/4	1-3/8
2-3/4	2-1/2	1-1/2
3	2-5/8	1-5/8
3-1/4	2-3/4	1-5/8
3-1/2	3	1-3/4
3-3/4	3-1/8	1-7/8
4	3-3/8	1-7/8
4-1/4	3-1/2	2
4-1/2	3-5/8	2-1/8
4-3/4	3-7/8	2-1/4
5	4	2-1/4

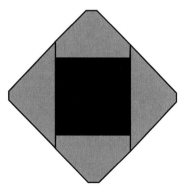

Hint: when cutting strip size it may be easier to cut 1/4ths than 1/8ths. You can round the strip size up to the nearest 1/4th.

Cut your "SnS®" in half. You will need to leave 1/4" seam allowance at the top (north) and bottom (south) sides of your "SnS®" when you trim up the corners. Cut like "Option 1" on the north and south side of your "SnS®". On the opposite side of your square, trim up to the point of the inside square. Put the tip of the line in the tip of the center square. Cut in half as shown.

To make these so they will match up against an Option #1 add 3/8" to cut center square size, then use regular "Square in a Square®" formula to get corner strip size.

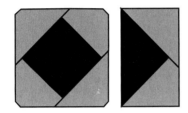

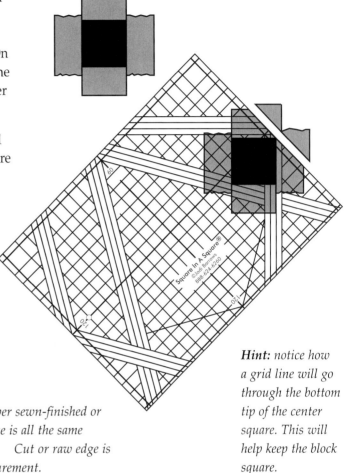

Magic Math™: Draw your pattern out on graph paper. Measure sewn center square and add 7/8" to the center square for cut size. Figure strip size as always.

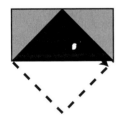

Hint: Remember sewn-finished or graph paper size is all the same measurement. Cut or raw edge is the same measurement.

Hint: notice how a grid line will go through the bottom tip of the center square. This will help keep the block square.

Chart for Option #3
Flying Geese

For Sewn Size of Rectangle Unit	Cut Center Square	Cut Strip Size
1 x 2	2-1/4	1-3/8
1-1/4 x 2-1/2	2-5/8	1-5/8
1-1/2 x 3	3	1-3/4
1-3/4 x 3-1/2	3-3/8	2
2 x 4	3-3/4	2-1/8
2-1/4 x 4-1/2	4	2-1/4
2-1/2 x 5	4-3/8	2-1/2
2-3/4 x 5-1/2	4-3/4	2-5/8
3 x 6	5-1/8	2-7/8

Hint: when using large Flying Geese this may be helpful. Before cutting your #3 in half, stay stitch 1/4" from the center cut lines on each side.

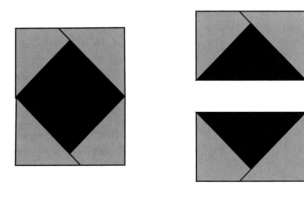

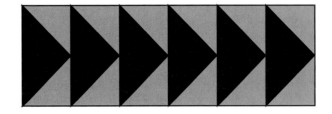

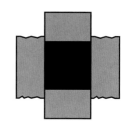

Cut all 4 sides up to the point. Cut in half again. It makes 4 squares with triangles! The "SnS®" squares can be cut to make half square triangles. There are two formulas for making the half square triangles. If you want half square triangles so that four of them sewn together make a unit the size of a "SnS®", **cut the center square 3/4" larger than** the center square of the full "SnS®". Cut the corner strips half the width of the center square. For example: The full square uses a cut square of 2-1/2" and corners strips 1-1/2" wide. The half square triangles are made with a 3-1/4" square (2-1/2" + 3/4") and corner strips of 1-5/8" (3-1/4" ÷ 2).

If you just want half square triangles and they don't have to match up with a full "SnS®", use the following formula. **Multiply the desired cut size of the half square triangle by 1.414 and add 1/2" to get the size of the center square.** Round to the nearest 1/8". The corner strips are half the width of the center square. For example: You want 3" half square triangles (finished size 2-1/2"). The center square is cut 4-3/4" or [(3" x 1.414) + 1/2"]. The corner strips are cut 2-3/8" (4-3/4" ÷ 2). Cut all four sides up to the point like the east west sides on Option #3. Next cut the square into quarters.

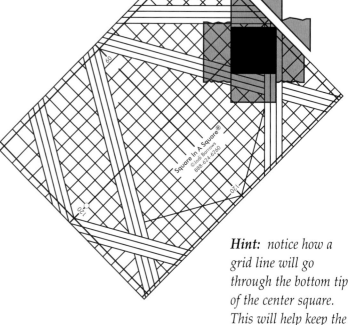

Hint: notice how a grid line will go through the bottom tip of the center square. This will help keep the block square.

To use the option charts you need to know the cut (raw) size or sewn size of the square unit.

 or

Then follow the measurements on the Option #4 chart.

Chart for Option #4
Half Square Triangles

For Sewn Size of 1/2 Square Triangle Unit	Cut Center Square	Cut Strip Size
1/2	2	1-1/4
1	2-5/8	1-1/2
1-1/4	3	1-3/4
1-1/2	3-3/8	2
1-3/4	3-5/8	2-1/8
2	4	2-1/4
2-1/4	4-3/8	2-1/2
2-1/2	4-3/4	2-5/8
2-3/4	5	2-3/4
3	5-1/2	3

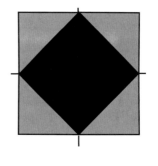

1/8 = .125	5/8 = .625
1/4 = .25	3/4 = .75
3/8 = .375	7/8 = .875
1/2 = .5	

12

Use any pattern in place of the solid middle square. Figure strip size as always.

When cutting your "SnS®", leave 1/4" seam allowance on all 4 sides of your square, don't sew or cut off the tip of the inside squares.

Use this math formula to find your strip size:

To find the strip size for the corner, measure center square..... Divide in half....Add 1/4"...... Cut strip this measurement for the next row to sew around your square.

Hint: *to save fabric, just sew a strip the length of the center square plus 1/2".*

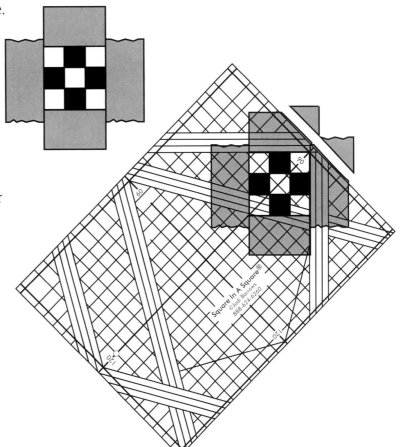

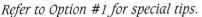

Refer to Option #1 for special tips.

Hint: *when cutting strip size it may be easier to cut 1/4ths than 1/8ths. You can round the strip size up to the nearest 1/4th.*

Hint: *remember sewn-finished or graph paper size are all the same size. Cut or raw edge is the same.*

$\mathcal{O}$PTION 11

Sew a "SnS®" block. Like Option #2 we will sew around the block twice. The first time we trim we will leave 1/4" seam allowance off the tip. The second row will be trimmed right up to the tip: Refer to Option #4 up to the tip trimming and tips.

Cut the block in half twice yielding 4 units.

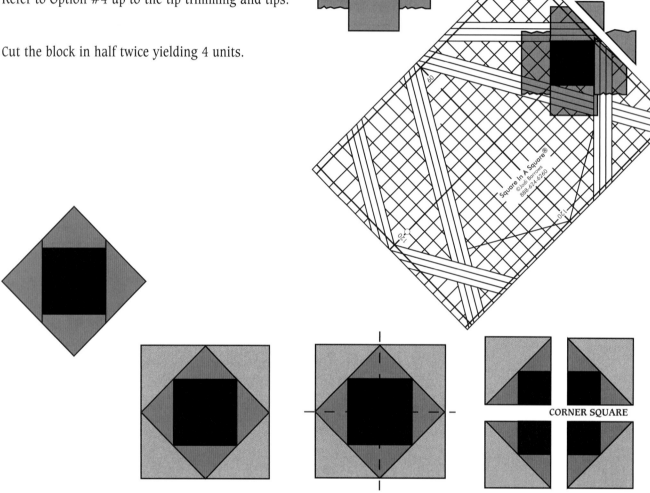

CORNER SQUARE

Chart for Option #11

Sewn Size of Corner Square	Cut for Center Square	Cut for First Row	Cut for Second Row
1	3	1-3/4	2-1/4
1-1/4	3-1/2	2	3
1-1/2	4	2-1/4	3-1/4
1-3/4	4-1/2	2-1/2	3-1/2
2	5	2-3/4	3-3/4
2-1/4	5-1/2	3	4-1/4
2-1/2	6	3-1/4	4-1/2
3	7	3-3/4	5-1/4

Math for Option #11: Draw your pattern on graph paper or know your sewn size of your corner square. Double that size and add 1" for the cut center square size of your "SnS®". Figure strip size as always.

Hint: *remember sewn-finished or graph paper size is all the same measurement. Cut or raw edge is the same measurement.*

Sew a "SnS®" block. Sew around the block the first time and trim up to the point of the center square. Use one line on the ruler (90°) and place it over the seam, right up to the point. Be careful not to trim off too much or too little. This is like Option #4 and #10.

Figure strip size as always and sew around the block again leaving 1/4" seam allowance off of the tip like Option #1. Your inside square will now be blunted.

Figure new strip size and sew around your block for the 3rd time. Trim up to the tip, same as above, like Option #4.

Cut in half, twice, edge to edge, making sure you have 1/4" seam allowance on inside blunted square. Yields 4 units.

Hint: notice how a grid line will go through the bottom tip of the center square. This will help keep the block square.

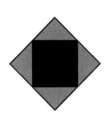 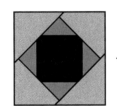 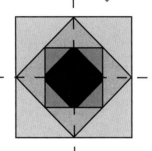

THIS CUT SIZE

Chart for Option #14

Cut Size of Square that will be 1/2 Square Triangles	Cut for Center Square	Cut for First Row	Cut for Second Row	Cut for Third Row
1	2	1-1/4	1-1/2	2-1/4
1-1/2	2-5/8	1-1/2	2	2-3/4
1-3/4	3	1-3/4	2-1/4	3
2	3-3/8	2	2-1/2	3-1/2
2-1/4	3-5/8	2-1/8	3	3-3/4
2-1/2	4	2-1/4	3-1/4	4-1/4
2-3/4	4-3/8	2-1/2	3-1/2	4-3/4
3	4-3/4	2-5/8	3-5/8	5
3-1/4	5	2-3/4	3-3/4	5-1/2
3-1/2	5-1/2	3	4-1/4	5-3/4

Math for Option #14: Draw your pattern out on graph paper. Measure the sewn size of your half square triangle. Multiply the desired cut size of that square triangle unit by 1.414, and add 1/2" to get the square size for the center square of your "SnS®". Round to the nearest 1/8". Figure corner strips as always.

For example: You want 3" half square triangles (finished size 2-1/2"). The center square is cut 4-3/4" or [(3" x 1.414) + 1/2"]. The corner strips are cut 2-3/8" (4-3/4" ÷ 2). Cut all four sides up to the point like the east and west sides on Option #3.

This new option is a mix of several options. You may choose anything to go in the center, to become the center square or unit. Try a pieced block, 4 patch, 9 patch, solid square...most anything will work. Next surround the center choice, like always, with the strip on each side of the center unit. Remember, only the center unit needs to be covered.

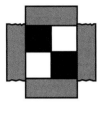  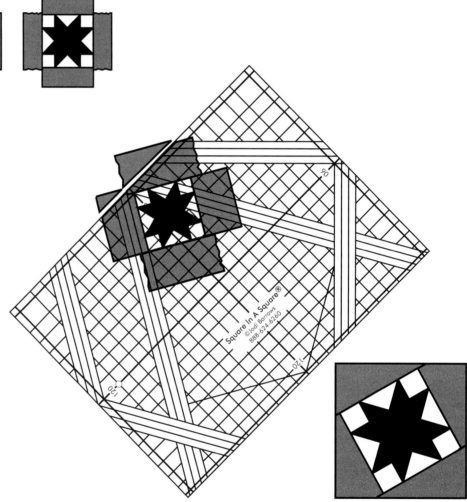

Place 60° angle over center unit. The 60° angle tip should lay over the tip of center unit, leaving 1/4" seam allowance off of the tip. Only one side of the ruler angle will line up with the seam below it. Trim all four corners, *rotate the block the same direction* as you trim it. All four corners should be turned clock wise or counter clockwise. This will create mirror images. Also be careful to always use the left side of the angle or the right when trimming all four corners. This will also create mirror image blocks. Practice with 2 blocks, cutting all four corners with the left, then the right side of the 60° angle on all four corners of the second block. This will help you see what you can create. The block will now start to twist. Sew around the block as many times as you need to design your block.

Hint: refer to option and option chart 1•2•5; it may help your designing

Hint: when the center unit is larger than a cut 5" or 6", 1/2" needs to be added, when figuring strip size, not the normal 1/4"

Hint: strip size may be rounded up for cutting to nearest 1/4".

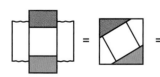 = = = 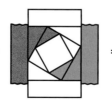 =  =

Keep sewing strips and trimming, block keeps twisting

BASIC DIAMOND CUTTING & SEWING

Substitute a 60° diamond for the center square. You will be creating with diamonds and long thin triangles. Cut the diamonds from a strip of fabric. Lay the 60° angle on a ruler along the horizontal edge of the strip. Trim the strip along the edge of the ruler. Continue to cut diamond segments the same width as the strip. Check the angle every 3-4 cuts to make sure it is still 60°, recutting if necessary.

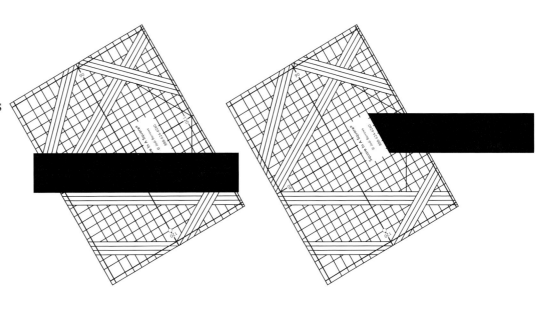

Add corner strips. Use the same formula for finding the width of the corner strips as used for squares (width of diamond strip ÷ 2 + 1/4"). Sew strips to the two opposite sides first. Trim even with the diamond.

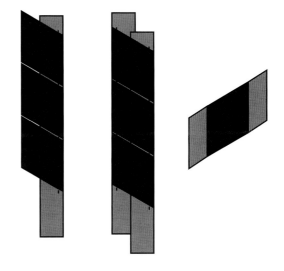

Sew corner strips to the remaining two sides.

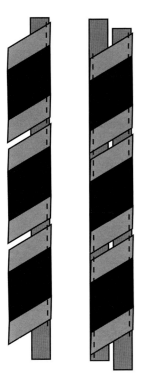

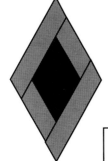

Hint: Remember sewn-finished or graph paper size is all the same measurement. Cut or raw edge is the same measurement.

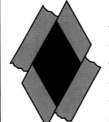

Hint: Short strips may be sewn to sides 3 & 4 to save fabric. I personally use short strips unless it is a miniature

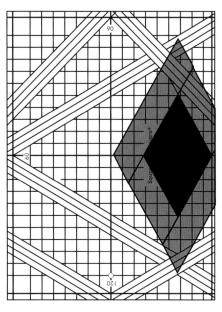

Cutting Option #18 is slightly different than the Option #7 diamond. Leave 1/4" at the sharp (60°) points of the diamond. Leave 1/8" at the other (120°) points. This is necessary to move the points and seam allowance for sharp points.

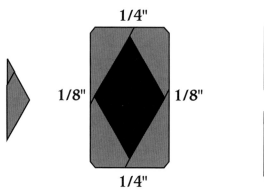

1/4"

1/8"   1/8"

1/4"

North

South

Hint: Review Option #7 for 1/4" trim on the 60° tip.

Hint: Notice how the center diamond cut strip size is almost always the exact measurement as the North or South cut size of the Canadian Geese. As the #18 units (CG) get larger the center diamond strip size grows smaller. When comparing the smaller #18 (CG) units the center strip size grows larger than the North or South of the CG.

Hint: To use the #18 chart you must know the cut or sewn size of the Canadian Geese rectangle unit required for design. Follow chart across for diamond strip size and surround strip size.

Hint: To slightly adjust size of final unit change diamond strip size slightly or seam allowance slightly or by adjusting the ruler on the final trim. Also shaving or "squaring up" the unit will alter the size.

Chart for Option #18 - Canadian Geese™

Cut Canadian Geese (CG)	Sewn Finished or Graph Paper Size (CG)	Cut Strip for Center Diamond	Cut Strip Size
1-1/4 x 1-1/8	3/4 x 5/8	1-3/8	1
1-1/2 x 1-1/4	1 x 3/4	1-1/2	1
1-3/4 x 1-1/2	1-1/4 x 1	1-3/4	1-1/8
2 x 1-3/4	1-1/2 x 1-1/4	2	1-1/4
2-1/4 x 2	1-3/4 x 1-1/2	2-1/4	1-3/8
2-1/2 x 2-1/4	2 x 1-3/4	2-1/2	1-1/2
2-3/4 x 2-1/2	2-1/4 x 2	2-3/4	1-5/8
3 x 2-5/8	2-1/2 x 2-1/4	2-7/8	1-3/4
3-1/4 x 2-7/8	2-3/4 x 2-3/8	3-1/4	1-7/8
3-1/2 x 3-1/8	3 x 2-5/8	3-3/8	2
3-3/4 x 3-3/8	3-1/4 x 2-7/8	3-1/2	2
4 x 3-1/2	3-1/2 x 3	3-3/4	2-1/8
4-1/4 x 3-3/4	3-3/4 x 3-1/4	4	2-1/4
4-1/2 x 4	4 x 3-1/2	4-1/4	2-3/8

Hint: The long side of the original uncut rectangle unit becomes the short side of the #18 CG. The short side of the original uncut rectangle or the North South side becomes the long side of the #18 CG.

Hint: Sewing a sample unit is always a good idea.

OPTION 19 - LONG THIN TRIANGLE

The Option #19 cut will create a blunt look on the block on the top and bottom, North and South.

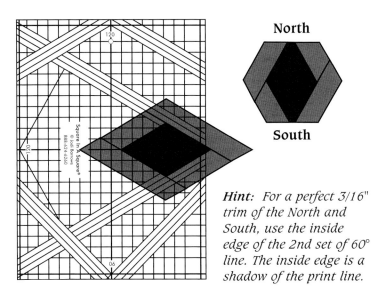

North

South

Hint: For a perfect 3/16" trim of the North and South, use the inside edge of the 2nd set of 60° line. The inside edge is a shadow of the print line.

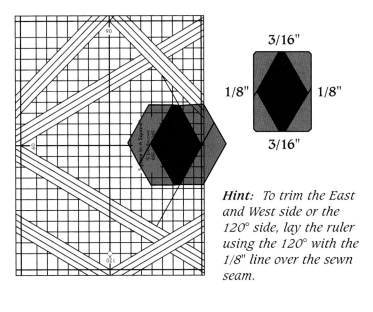

3/16"

1/8"   1/8"

3/16"

Hint: To trim the East and West side or the 120° side, lay the ruler using the 120° with the 1/8" line over the sewn seam.

Hint: Notice the S or F by some measurements with the trimming requirements for the Option #19 being a 3/16 on the North + South side. It is difficult to create an exact and easy measurement. 3/16 is 3 or 4 threads. That is the thickness of a cutting line on a tool. The S means scant cut. The F equals a full cut. To make a full cut it would be on the outside of the cutting line to make the size larger. Of course providing that your cutting and sewing is perfect. Remember the size of your units depend on 3 things: the size of your center unit of the option, your seam allowance all figured on a scant or skinny 1/4", and lastly, the way you lay the cutting tool on the sewn piece. Are you cutting with the line to create a scant or skinny cut or a full and fat cut. Have fun with which ever you do. The perfection is here for you Rocket Science quilters. The technqiue is forgiving for the Smoking Needle quilter.

Hint: To use the #19 chart you must know the cut or sewn size of the rectangle unit required for design. Follow chart across for diamond strip size and surround strip size.

Hint: To slightly adjust size of final unit change diamond strip size slightly or seam allowance slightly or by adjusting the ruler on the final trim. Also shaving or "squaring up" the unit will alter the size.

Hint: The long side of the original uncut rectangle unit stays the long side of the new #19 Long Thin Triangles.

Hint: Sewing a sample unit is always a good idea.

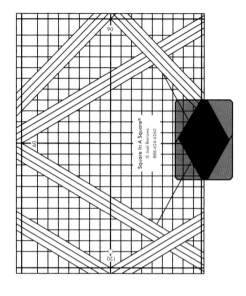

Next, cut the unit in half top to bottom and side to side. Use the 1/8" line on the 120° side of the ruler. This will allow the perfect amount of fabric in the seam allowance.

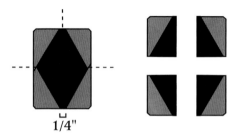

1/4"

Hint: the blunt North and South should be a perfect 1/4" area.

Hint: to double check your perfect 1/4" seam allowance on the final four cut units, lay ruler on the unit so the far right corner is on the fabric unit at the sewn diagonal seam corner. Seam should run through ruler intersection on far right corner.

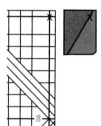

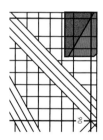

Hint: The four Option #19 units will have two that are mirror images of the other two. The two that match are kitty corner of each other.

Chart for Option #19
Long Thin Triangles (LTT)

Cut Size of individual Long Thin Triangle	Sewn Size of individual Long Thin Triangle	Cut Size of Center Diamond Strip	Cut Size of Surround Strip for Center Diamond
1^F x 7/8	1/2^F x 3/8	1-3/4	1-1/8
1-1/4^F x 1	3/4^F x 1/2	2	1-1/4
1-1/2^F x 1-1/8	1^F x 5/8	2-1/4	1-3/8
1-3/4^S x 1-1/4	1-1/4^S x 3/4	2-1/2	1-1/2
2 x 1-3/8	1-1/2 x 7/8	2-3/4	1-5/8
2-1/8 x 1-1/2	1-5/8 x 1	2-7/8	1-3/4
2-3/8^S x 1-5/8	1-7/8^F x 1-1/8	3-1/4	1-7/8
2-5/8^F x 1-3/4	2-1/8^F x 1-1/4	3-3/8	2
2-7/8^F x 1-7/8	2-3/8^F x 1-3/8	3-1/2	2
3-1/8 x 2	2-5/8 x 1-1/2	3-3/4	2-1/8
3-1/4^F x 2-1/8	2-3/4 x 1-5/8	4	2-1/4
3-1/2^F x 2-1/4	3 x 1-3/4	4-1/4	2-3/8

Short side or N or S / Long side

OPTION 20 - ROOF TOP TRIANGLES

The Option #20 cut will create a blunt look on the block on the top and bottom, North and South.

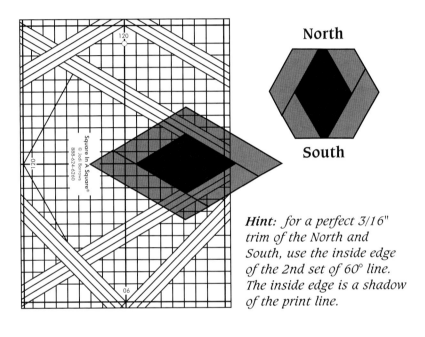

North

South

Hint: for a perfect 3/16" trim of the North and South, use the inside edge of the 2nd set of 60° line. The inside edge is a shadow of the print line.

Hint: *Notice the S or F by some measurements with the trimming requirements for the Option #19 being a 3/16 on the North + South side. It is difficult to create an exact and easy measurement. 3/16 is 3 or 4 threads. That is the thickness of a cutting line on a tool. The S means scant cut. The F equals a full cut. To make a full cut it would be on the outside of the cutting line to make the size larger. Of course providing that your cutting and sewing is perfect. Remember the size of your units depend on 3 things: the size of your center unit of the option, your seam allowance all figured on a scant or skinny 1/4", and lastly, the way you lay the cutting tool on the sewn piece. Are you cutting with the line to create a scant or skinny cut or a full and fat cut. Have fun with which ever you do. The perfection is here for you Rocket Science quilters. The technqiue is forgiving for the Smoking Needle quilter.*

Hint: *To use the #19 chart you must know the cut or sewn size of the rectangle unit required for design. Follow chart across for diamond strip size and surround strip size.*

Hint: *To slightly adjust size of final unit change diamond strip size slightly or seam allowance slightly or by adjusting the ruler on the final trim. Also shaving or "squaring up" the unit will alter the size.*

Hint: *The long side of the original uncut rectangle unit stays the long side of the new #19 Long Thin Triangles.*

Hint: *Sewing a sample unit is always a good idea.*

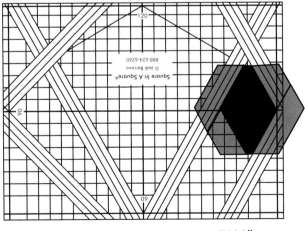

Hint: To trim the East and West side lay 120° with the 1/4" line over the seam. You must leave 1/4" from the point. This is the same cut as Opt. #7.

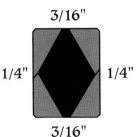

3/16"

1/4"   1/4"

3/16"

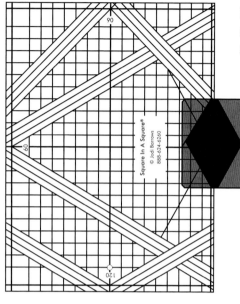

Next, cut the unit in half top to bottom. Use the 1/8" line on the 120° side of the ruler. This will allow the perfect amount of fabric in the seam allowance.

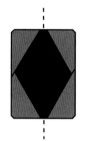 

Hint: the blunt North and South should be a perfect 1/4" area.

Hint: to double check your perfect 1/4" seam allowance on the final two cut units, lay ruler on the unit so the far right corner is on the fabric unit at the sewn diagonal seam corner. Seam should run through ruler intersection on far right corner.

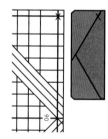

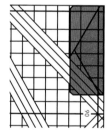

Chart for Option #20
Roof Top Triangles (RTT)

Cut Size of individual Roof Top Rectangle	Sewn Size of individual Roof Top Rectangle	Cut Size of Center Diamond Strip	Cut Size of Surround Strip for Center Diamond
1-1/4 x 3/4	3/4 x 1/4	1-3/8	1
1-5/8 x 7/8	1-1/8 x 3/8	1-1/2	1
2 x 1	1-1/2 x 1/2	1-3/4	1-1/8
2-1/2 x 1^F	2 x 1/2^F	2	1-1/4
3 x 1-1/4	2-1/2 x 3/4	2-1/4	1-3/8
3-1/2 x 1-3/8	3 x 7/8	2-1/2	1-1/2
4 x 1-1/2^F	3-1/2 x 1	2-3/4	1-5/8
4-1/4^F x 1-5/8	3-3/4 x 1-1/8	2-7/8	1-3/4
5 x 1-7/8	4-1/2 x 1-3/8	3-1/4*	1-7/8
5-1/4 x 2^S	4-3/4 x 1-1/2	3-3/8*	2
5-1/2 x 2	5 x 1-1/2	3-1/2*	2
6 x 2-1/8	5-1/2 x 1-7/8	3-3/4	2-1/8

*Notice how some of the diamond strip sizes are only 1/8" apart in size. This makes the long side of the roof top change, but not the short side. If you need a size not on the chart, find the closest one on the chart and adjust the diamond strip size up or down to create the desired size

Homestead Star
79" x 92"

Mrs. Sewell's Star
110" x 110"

Peddler's Choice -
Mr. Skelly's Quilt
67" x 75"

Split Bear Paw
73" x 92"

Monkey
Tails
63" x 74"

Lickety Split
Anna's Quilt
50" x 60"

Timber Trails
Grandpa's Quilt
63" x 63"

Abby's Basket Sampler
54" x 69"

Indian Blanket
76" x 88"

Emma's Crossroads
89" x 105"

Setting Triangle Chart

Anytime you set a block on point, it will make the block look more intricate. Even a simple block can achieve more pizzazz by setting on the angle. When you choose to set a block on point it puts your quilt top on the diagonal. The quilt is sewn together in rows, on the diagonal. The rows are finished on each end with triangle units. Two opposite corners of the quilt top will need to have corner triangle units sewn to those two rows. The other 2 corner triangle units are sewn as a part of that diagonal row. Remember, we work with two measurements of a block: 1) Sewn-finished or graph paper size, and 2) cut or raw edge unit or block.

This chart will help you know the corner triangle unit and side setting triangle square units. If the size you require is not on the chart, then bump up to the next larger size. You will have room to trim it up perfect. And remember, all of us have our own private sewing and cutting measurements, even our sewing machines have their own private measurements!

Side Setting Triangle Units

Side triangles are created by cutting a square and then cutting it in half twice diagonally. This square will create 4 triangle units that will be the side triangle units.

Corner Setting Triangle Units

Corner triangles are required for each of the 4 corners of the quilt top. One square creates 2 triangle units. Each quilt top will require 2 squares for the 4 corners.

Sewn Finished or Graph Paper Size Block	Cut Square for Side Triangle Units	Cut Square for Corner Triangle Units
2"	4-1/8"	2-3/8"
3"	5-1/2"	3"
4"	7"	3-3/4"
5"	8-3/8"	4-1/2"
6"	9-3/4"	5-1/8"
7"	11-1/4"	5-7/8"
8"	12-5/8"	6-5/8"
9"	14"	7-1/4"
10"	15-1/2"	8"
12"	18-1/4"	9-3/8"

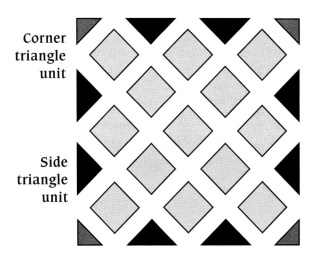

Corner triangle unit

Side triangle unit

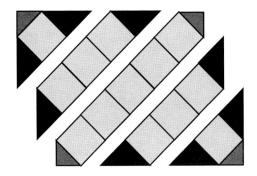

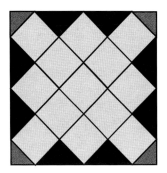

How to Square Up Your Quilt:

Lay your quilt on a smooth, flat area. Fold the short ends to the middle of the quilt. Do the edges all lay even? Is the middle the same size as the top and bottom? If it is not more than an inch, you have done well. Pat yourself on the back. If not, you need to ease or ooch some more. You may have to go deeper into the border to get it corrected. On the other hand, if it doesn't bother you, it doesn't bother me. Better luck next time.

How to Check for Square Corners on Your Quilt:

Lay your quilt out as described above. Do your corners have a true 90° edge when measured with a ruler? You may trim up to 1/4" without effecting your borders, more than that can cause odd border shapes and are noticeable to the eye. Borrow your husband's T square, if it helps, or use a ruler with the 45° line marked to help make miters.

All About Binding By Machine or Hand:

Binding is the finishing part. It makes a double layer around the edges of the quilt, keeping all 3 layers inside it. It can be done by machine or by hand. I cut most of mine 2-1/2" wide for large quilts and 2-1/4" for small. If machine binding (use a walking foot) is your choice, start on the back first. If by hand, start on the front. Follow pictures for "how to". Don't be afraid of those corners. They are not that hard.

Binding: Trim backing and batting even with the quilt edge. Make sure corners are square. Use a ruler and a rotary cutter. You can check to see if your quilt is square by folding the ends to the middle. The edges should all be even with each other.

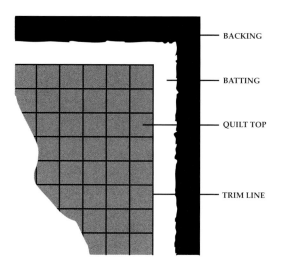

Straight of the grain binding is OK for most projects. If this is a big quilt, a contest or a Judged or Jury show quilt, use bias binding.

Trim ends at a 45° angle and sew binding in a long, continuous strip.

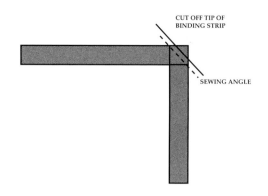

Step 1: Sew binding along edge of quilt, all edges even. Leave about 8" of binding loose at the starting point along the side of the quilt.

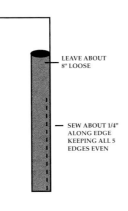

LEAVE ABOUT 8" LOOSE

SEW ABOUT 1/4" ALONG EDGE KEEPING ALL 5 EDGES EVEN

Step 2: Turn the binding at corner – stop 1/4" from bottom of quilt – backstitch – pull binding back up and pin. Lay binding back over bottom edge of quilt with a 45° mitered corner.

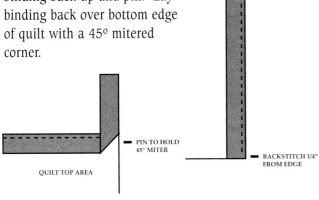

PIN TO HOLD 45° MITER

QUILT TOP AREA

BACKSTITCH 1/4" FROM EDGE

Step 3: Start stitching 1/4" from both sides of the corner. Be careful not to catch the fullness of the mitered corner.

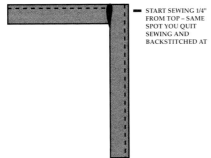

START SEWING 1/4" FROM TOP – SAME SPOT YOU QUIT SEWING AND BACKSTITCHED AT

Continue to sew around all 4 sides of quilt.

Step 4: To connect both ends, stop sewing about 10" from starting point – pin binding and quilt to center point and clip both binding strips.

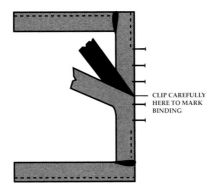

CLIP CAREFULLY HERE TO MARK BINDING

Step 5: Lay top binding over to the right – open it flat – face up. Bring bottom piece up – face down – connect clipped points and pin. Start sewing at left top corner of binding and sew down using a 45° angle to bottom right. Clipped points should line up evenly. Trim 1/4" from sewn line.

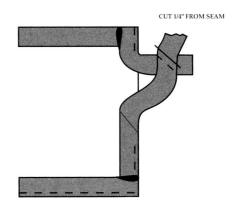

CUT 1/4" FROM SEAM

Step 6: After trimmed edges are off, it should lay flat against the quilt. Sew the binding down to quilt.

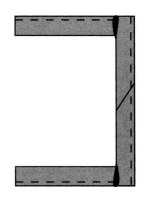

Step 7: Turn the binding over the edge of the quilt, keeping it smooth and tight. Blind stitch by hand or sew down using the sewing machine. If using the machine, attach the walking foot and slowly stitch down the binding very close to the edge. Use a stiletto and invisible thread.

Hint: remember the video shows the binding technique at the very end.

Split Bear Paw

73" x 92" • Advanced

The Split Bear Paw is a unique version of the traditional block. This 15" sewn block will go together quickly and not be a bear to make! You will learn Option #4 half square triangle units and the long thin triangles of Option #19 from the diamond units.

About Fabric:

We use the Leaving Riverton and Liz's Mercantile Fabric. If you wish to create your quilt with the same fabrics, follow the numbers below. Otherwise use the total amount of fabric listed.

I always figure healthy fabric amounts and round up to 1/4 yard increments.

Liz's Mercantile

Light #59431
Dark   #59433

Dark in block – 3 yds
Light in block – 3 yds
9 Patch Unit – 3/4 yd dark
             1/2 yd light
Sashings Light – 3 yd
Border 1 – 1 1/2 yd
Binding – 1 yd
Backing – 6 yds
For individual fabric yardage look at the amounts from each cutting section.

Cutting

Small Option #4 - Half square triangle units
1/2 yd cut 3 strips – 5 1/2" into 12 center squares
                          light
1 yd cut 8 strips – 3" for surround strips dark
Large Option #4 - Half square triangle units
1/2 yd cut 3 strips – 6 1/8" into 12 center squares
                          light
1 yd cut 8 strips – 3 1/2" for surround strips dark
Option #19 - Long thin triangle units
1 yd cut 6 strips – 4 1/4" into 48 center diamonds
                          units dark
1 3/4" yd cut 24 strips – 2 1/2" for surround strips
                          light

Cutting Continued

Inside Block Setting Square –
Cut 12 - 2 1/2" squares
3/4 yd Sashing –
Cut 8 strips - 2 1/2" crosscut into
                 48 - 2 1/2" x 7" rectangles
9 Patch Sections –
Cut 5 - 2" strips of light or 96 - 2" squares
Cut 6 - 2" strips of dark or 120 - 2" squares
Sashing Border 1
Cut 16 - 5" strips of light into 31 - 5" x 15 1/2" rectangles. (always measure your completed units before cutting any sashing)
Border 2
Cut 9 - 5" strip

Sewing

Step 1 – Sew 12 – Option #4 half square triangle units using 5 1/2" center squares and 3" surround strips.

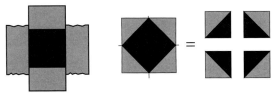

Step 2 – Sew 12 Option #4 half square triangle units using 5 5/8" center square and 3 1/2" strip.

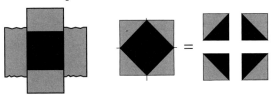

Step 3 – Sew 48 diamond units 4 1/4" and 2 1/2" surround strips trim into Option #19 long thin triangles. Watch the trimming *carefully.*

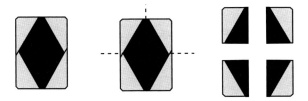

Step 4 – Sew block together using 2 1/2" squares and 2 1/2" x 7" sashing.

Step 5 – Strip piece 2" strips of light and dark colors into 3 strip strata's - crosscut using the 9 patch ruler into 2" sections. Sew 24 - 9 patch units - (cut 5" units)

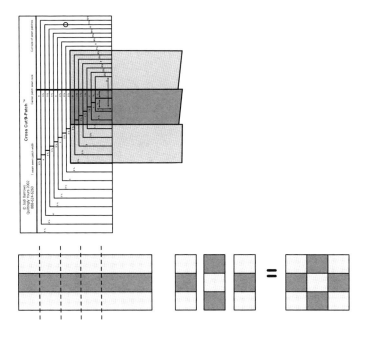

Step 6 – Sew 9 Patch blocks and sashing 5" x 15 1/2" - according to picture layout.

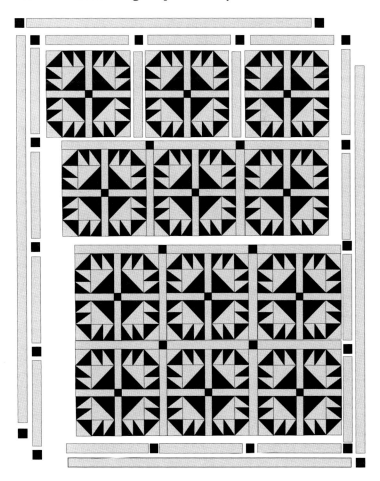

31

Mrs. Sewell's Star

110" x 110" • Advanced

Mrs. Sewells Star is unusual in the fact that the Ohio Star setting block is the focal point of the quilt. You will learn Option #1 and Option #3 for the small star and Option #4 half square triangles for the large 12" block. This design is a close sister to a feathered star.

About Fabric:

We use the Leaving Riverton and Liz's Mercantile Fabric. If you wish to create your quilt with the same fabrics, follow the numbers below. Otherwise use the total amount of fabric listed.

I always figure healthy fabric amounts and round up to 1/4 yard increments.

Dark 1 - Red   #59343   #59348
                      #59434   #59316
                                    3 1/2 yds Total

Dark 2 - Brown	#59405	1 1/4 yds
Dark 3 - Black	#59407	1 yd
Light or Background	#59402	10 yds
Border Black Flower	#59428	
Binding	#59434	2 yds
Backing	#59434	12 yds

For individual fabric yardage look at the amounts from each cutting section.

Cutting

Block 1

Ohio Star - small Option #1 center
1 Fat Q - cut 2 strips - 1 7/8" into 17 center square of dark or red
1/4 yd - cut 5 strips - 1 1/4" surround strips of light print

Ohio Star - Flying Geese - Star points Option #3
1/4 yd - cut 2 strips - 2 1/4" into 34 center squares of brown
1/2 yd - cut 9 strips - 1 1/2 " surround strips of black

Ohio Star - Corner Square
1/4 yd - cut 4 strips 1 3/4" into 68 squares of brown

Block 2 - Option #4 - Half square triangle units
1/3 yd - cut 3 strips - 3 1/8" into 30 dark 3 or black center squares
2/3 yd - cut 10 strips - 1 3/4" surround strips of light
1/2 yd - cut 6 strips - 1 7/8" for solid block squares 120 light

2/3 yd - cut 12 strips - 2" for Option #5 surround strips light
2/3 yd - cut 12 strips - 2" for Option #5 surround strips dark 2 - brown

Block 3 - Option #4 - Half square triangles
1/3 yd - cut 3 strips 3 1/8" into 34 dark 1 or red center squares
2/3 yd - cut 10 strips - 1 3/4" surround strips of light
1/4 yd - cut 3 strips 1 7/8" for solid block squares 60 light
1/4 yd - cut 3 strips 1 7/8" for solid block squares 60 dark 1 - red
1 1/3 yd - cut 24 strips 2" for Option #5 surround strip light

Block 4 - Large 12" sewn block
2 1/3 yd - cut 9 strips 8 1/2" for 36 squares
1 3/4 yd - cut 17 strips 4" of light for cut 120 - 4" center squares
2 3/4 yd - cut 81 strips 2 1/4" of dark 1 or red for surround strips
1/2 yd - cut 5 strips 2 1/2" of light into 78 - 2 1/2" squares

Sashing
2 3/4 yd - cut 21 strips 4 1/2" into 12 - 4 1/2" x 16 1/2"
                                    12 - 4 1/2" x 12 1/2"
                                    12 - 4 1/2" x 8 1/2"
                                    55 - 4 1/2" x 4 1/2"

Sewing

Step 1 – Sew 30 Option #1s using 1 7/8" dark 1 or red center square and 1 1/4" light surround strips.

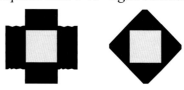

Step 2 – Sew 60 Option #3s using 2 1/4" dark 2 or brown center square and 1 1/2" dark 3 or black surround strips.

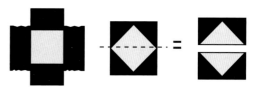

Step 3 –

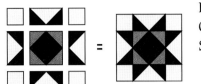

Block size
Cut 4¹/₂"
Sewn 4"

Step 4 - Block 2 - Sew 30 Option #4 half square triangles using 3¹/₈" dark 3 center squares and 1³/₄" light surround strips.

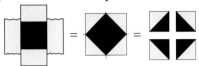

Sew 60 units adding 1⁷/₈" light squares. Watch color placement.

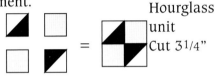

Hourglass unit
Cut 3¹/₄"

Step 5 - The hourglass unit now is Option #5 put it in the middle and surround with 2" surround strips of dark 2 and light. Watch color placement carefully.

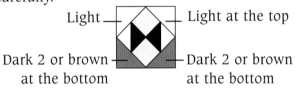

Light ——— ——— Light at the top
Dark 2 or brown — — Dark 2 or brown
at the bottom   at the bottom
Cut 4¹/₂" Block

Step 6 Block 3 - Sew 30 Option #4 half square triangles using 3¹/₈" dark 1, red center squares and light 1³/₄" surround strips

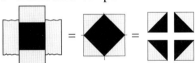

Sew 60 units adding 1⁷/₈" light square and 1⁷/₈" dark 1 red squares. Watch color placement.

Hourglass unit
Cut 3¹/₄"

Step 7 - The hour glass unit now is Option #5 put it in the middle and surround with 2" surround strips light. Watch color placement carefully.

Cut 4¹/₂"
Block

Step 8 - Sew 162 Option #4 half square triangle using 4" center squares and red surround strips.

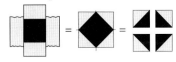

Sew block together using 8¹/₂" center square and 2¹/₂" corner squares.

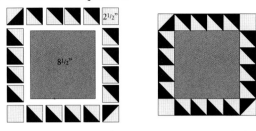

Step 9 - Sew together in sections and then rows.

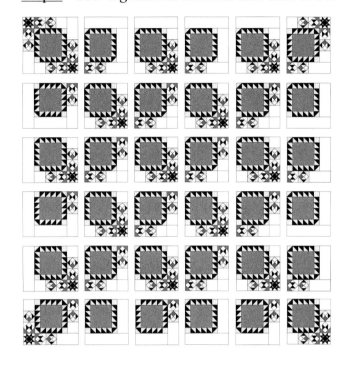

Step 10 - Border with a cut 5¹/₂" dark strip.

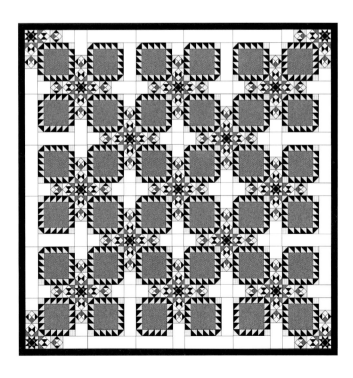

33

Peddler's Choice - Mr. Skelly's Quilt

Really simple is the name of the game for this block, traditionally known as the *Cracker Box*. Option #5 is put anything in the middle, just sew 3 equal size strips together into a strata and cross cut into a square. This becomes the center square unit that you sew around with the surround strips. Sew as many as you wish to create the size of quilt you like. These blocks are 8" sewn - 8½" cut.

Use a variety of colors, make really scrappy or use just a few colors for a coordinated look.

About Fabric:

We use the Leaving Riverton and Liz's Mercantile Fabric. If you wish to create your quilt with the same fabrics, follow the numbers below. Otherwise use the total amount of fabric listed. I always figure healthy fabric amounts and round up to ¼ yard increments.

Liz's Mercantile

Black Wreath	#59345	2½ yds
Tan Stars	#59435	3 yds
Red Button Weed	#59404	3 yds

Leaving Riverton

Green Star Trail	#59326	2½ yds

Binding – ¾ yd
Backing – 5 yds
For individual fabric yardage look at the amounts from each cutting section.

Cutting

Center Rectangle

Units - ¾ yd cut 6 strips - 2⅜" black
⠀⠀⠀⠀ ¾ yd cut 6 strips - 2⅜" red
⠀⠀⠀⠀ ¾ yd cut 6 strips - 2⅜" green
⠀⠀⠀⠀ 1 yd cut 9 strips - 2⅜" background tan

Surround

Strips - ¾ yd cut 7 strips - 3½" black
⠀⠀⠀⠀ ¾ yd cut 7 strips - 3½" red
⠀⠀⠀⠀ ¾ yd cut 7 strips - 3½" green
⠀⠀⠀⠀ 2 yd cut 16 strips - 3½" background tan

Borders

¾ yd cut 7 strips - 3½" red
½ yd cut 7 strips - 2½" green or 232 - 2½" squares from left over fabric above or 101 - 2½" squares. Try the 4 patch ruler or 9 patch ruler for quick and accurate units. If you want to strip the squares you will need about 14 - 2½" strips for the square border. If you add ¼ yd to each of the above totals of fabric.

¾ yd cut 7 strips - 3½" black wreath
½ yd cut 8 strips - 2" red

Sewing

Step 1 – Sew 3 equal width strips of 2⅜" together. Sew the darker on outside edge of lighter center. This is a 6⅛" wide strata. Cross cut into 6⅛" squares.

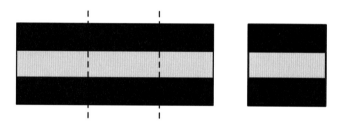

Repeat for each color combination for 14 black, 14 red, and 13 green. If you want these in the border sew 2 extra in black and 2 extra in green.

Step 2 – Sew 3½" background tan surround strips on each square, matching color correctly.

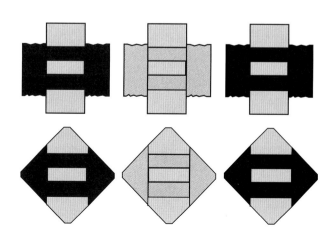

34

Step 3 – Sew unit together 6 across and 7 down. Use color placement

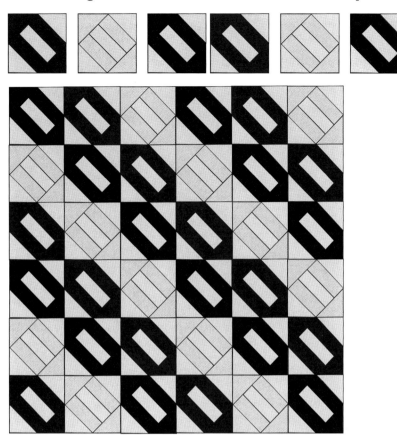

Step 4 – Border your quilt simply with large strips or use the left over fabric from above steps to make the small square sections and 8" blocks in the corners.

Border 1 - 3$\frac{1}{2}$" red
Border 2 - 2$\frac{1}{2}$" squares
Border 3 - 3$\frac{1}{2}$" black
Border 4 - 2" red

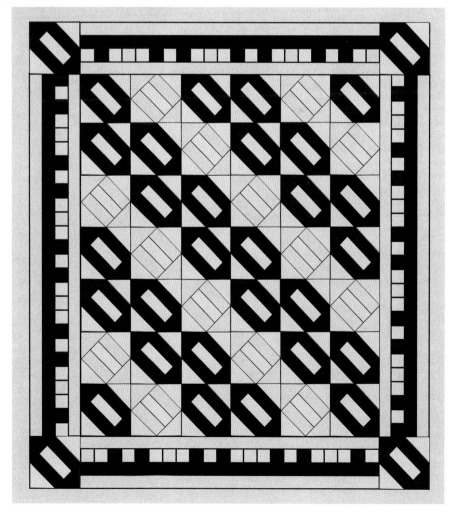

50" x 60" • **Beginners**

Lickety Split is a wonderful design using the Option #16 the twist. We used only 2 colors with an accent border color. Sew 40 with one color combo and the other 40 with reverse color combo Lickety Split you will be complete. One of my test students did the entire quilt top in 6 hours! The cutting for strips for the options to the last border! Yes, Lickety Split is a good name for this great quilt. Block size 4½" sewn - 5" cut.

About Fabric:

We use the Leaving Riverton and Liz's Mercantile Fabric. If you wish to create your quilt with the same fabrics, follow the numbers below. Otherwise use the total amount of fabric listed.

I always figure healthy fabric amounts and round up to ¼ yard increments.

Liz's Mercantile
Blue Star	#59433	1¾ yd
Light with Blue words	#59349	1¾ yd
Blue Words Large Border	#59346	1¼ yd

Leaving Riverton
Blue Vine Accent Border	#59339	½ yd
Binding	#59346	½ yd
Backing	#59426	3¼ yd

For individual fabric yardage look at the amounts from each cutting section.

Cutting

Option #16 - Color Combo A
½ yd Blue Star
Cut 4 strips into 40 - 4" center squares
1¼ yd Light Blue Words
Cut 18 strips 2¼" surround strips

Option #16 - Color Combo B (Reverse above)
½ yd Light Blue Words
Cut 4 strips into 40 - 4" center squares
1¼ yd Blue Star
Cut 18 strips 2¼" surround strips

Borders
½ yd cut 6 - 2" strips accent border
1¼ yd cut 6 - 6" strips darker border

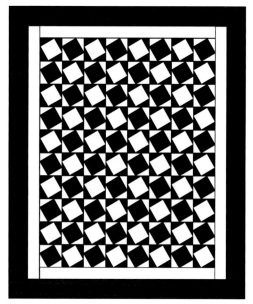

Sewing

Step 1 – Sew 40 - Option #16 twist squares using 4" centers and 2¼" surround strips. Repeat for 40 opposite color combo.

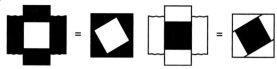

Step 2 – Sew in rows 8 across and 10 down.

Border with accent color border 1 strip. Use a wider and darker second border.

Monkey Tails - Anna's Quilt

63" x 74" • Beginners

Monkey Tails is a fast quilt. It just repeats a solid square with the Option #16 twist. Any size of block or quilt can be made so quickly and accurately. When you make a scrap quilt you divide the fabric color into values, of light, medium or dark. Many different mediums can fall into the dark category. A total amount of yardage will be given for each value.

About Fabric:

We use the Leaving Riverton and Liz's Mercantile Fabric. If you wish to create your quilt with the same fabrics, follow the numbers below. Otherwise use the total amount of fabric listed.

I always figure healthy fabric amounts and round up to 1/4 yard increments.

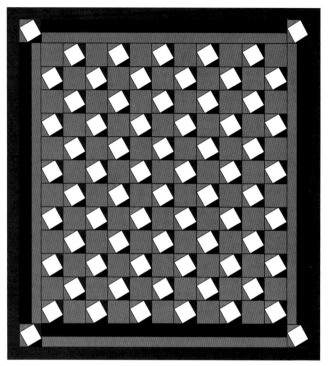

Leaving Riverton Darks and Mediums

#59329	#59328	#59327	#59326
#59321	#59320	#59317	#59316
#59301			

Leaving Riverton Lights   #59331

Liz's Mercantile Darks

#59432	#59433	#59434	#59342
#59343	#59345	#59346	#59428
#59348	#59350	#59404	#59405
#59407	#59436		

Fabric Requirements
4 yds of mixed darks and mediums for setting squares and Option #16 surround strips.
1 yd mixed lights for Option #16 center.

Borders 1 - Gold Star Trail	#59329	1/2 yd
Borders 2 - Gold Check	#59309	3/4 yd
Borders 3 - Green Star Trail	#59326	1 yd

Binding – 1 yd
Backing – 5 yds

For individual fabric yardage look at the amounts from each cutting section.

Cutting

Cut 10 strips - 51/4" setting squares into 66 solid setting squares

Option #16 - Cut 7 strips 4" into 70 - 4" center squares of light
Cut 30 strips - 21/4" of dark and medium surround strips for Option #16 or
280 - 21/4" x 41/4" scrap piece
Hint: Measurement includes the 4 corner units

Borders
21/2" cut 6 strips - Border 1
31/2" cut 6 strips - Border 2
31/2" cut 7 strips - Border 3

Sewing

Step 1 – Sew 70 - Option #16 units using 4" light center squares and 21/4" surround strips of dark. Sew scrappy, use different colors on each side.

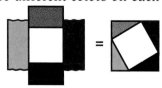

Hint: Sew 4 extra for border

37

<u>Step 2</u> – Sew Option #16 units to solid dark squares 11 across by 12 down. Sew into rows and then the rows together.

If you wish to make this a Star Quilt; use a light solid square in the odd rows.

When attaching the border, remember to measure your quilt top for your accurate size.

<u>Step 3</u> – Sew the 6 border 1 strips together in a long row. Repeat for border 2. Next sew the two together. Press and sew to two opposite sides of the quilt.
For the other 2 sides measure quilt and cut to the length, then add the Option #16 corner units to each end. Sew to quilt. Sew border 3 to each side.

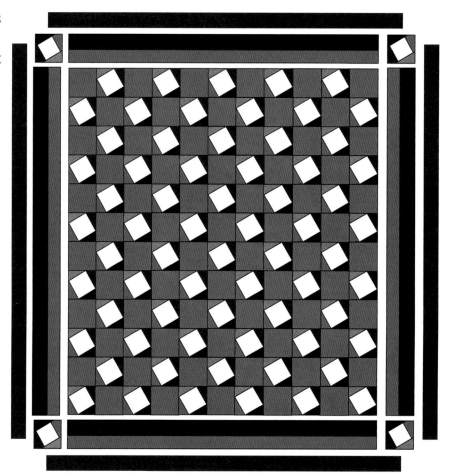